NIBBLES

For Liz & Matt, love always, Emma x

LITTLE TIGER PRESS LTD,
an imprint of the Little Tiger Group
1 Coda Studios, 189 Munster Road, London SW6 6AW
www.littletiger.co.uk

First published in Great Britain 2019
This edition published 2020
Text and illustrations copyright © Emma Yarlett 2019

ISBN 978-1-78881-401-0 · LTP/1800/3132/0420 · Printed in China
10 9 8 7 6 5 4 3 2 1

I love books.

Books **BIG** and books small.
But books about monsters
are my favourite.
Especially books about . . .

. . . book monsters.

Uh-oh!
There's a crunching, munching
book monster on the loose!
Can you find him?

Where did
he go?

Nibbles?

Nibbles!
There he is!
And he's
nibbled his
way into my
favourite
fact book.
Follow that
book monster!

MY FASCINATING
BOOK of FACTS

EMMETT LARAY

GOSH, it's hot in here. **OI, NIBBLES!** Get out of my book! You're making a monstrous mess.

The sun is roughly 15,000,000 degrees Celsius! That's HOT!

I'm a ₌SUPER₌ STAR!

SUN.

The sun is a big star found at the centre of our solar system. Eight planets, including the earth, circle around it. The sun is **92.96 million miles** away from our planet, which is the perfect distance to keep us alive; we never get too hot, or too cold. It is also VERY BIG, nearly 110 times wider than the earth!

In 1969, Apollo 11 was the first manned space rocket to land on the moon. Neil Armstrong was the first astronaut to walk on the moon's surface.

MOON

Just as the earth circles around the sun, so the moon orbits the earth. The moon is around **238,857 miles** away from our planet and has lots of craters and mountains. The moon might look round to the naked eye but it's actually egg-shaped. We see the widest face, which points towards the earth.

DOGS

It's believed that friendly, domesticated dogs are descended from a ferocious species of prehistoric wolf. This could account for their incredible hearing (which is four times better than a human's) and fantastic sense of smell. A dog's whiskers are so sensitive that they feel vibrations in the air, which warns the dog of any threat.

CATS

Cats were first domesticated in ancient Egypt from a species of wild cat. Lions, tigers and leopards are part of the cat family and are referred to as 'big cats'. Lions live in families (or 'prides') of around 15 members. They are intelligent pack hunters and their ROAR is nearly 25 times louder than an industrial lawn mower!

IMAGES

NIBBLES freed the DRAGON!

This won't end well!

Since the dawn of time, humans have drawn pictures to show their feelings and ideas. Images add visual meaning to stories. Some of the earliest paintings ever found were made by cavemen on cave walls! Nowadays, people use many things to create a picture, from paints and brushes, to computers and cameras.

BOOK MONSTERS make the TASTIEST SNACK!

WORDS

The World of Colour

Yikes!
Time to go!

Lemy·A·Matter

Words help us explain the world around us and describe how we see things like people and shapes. They are even used to explain colours

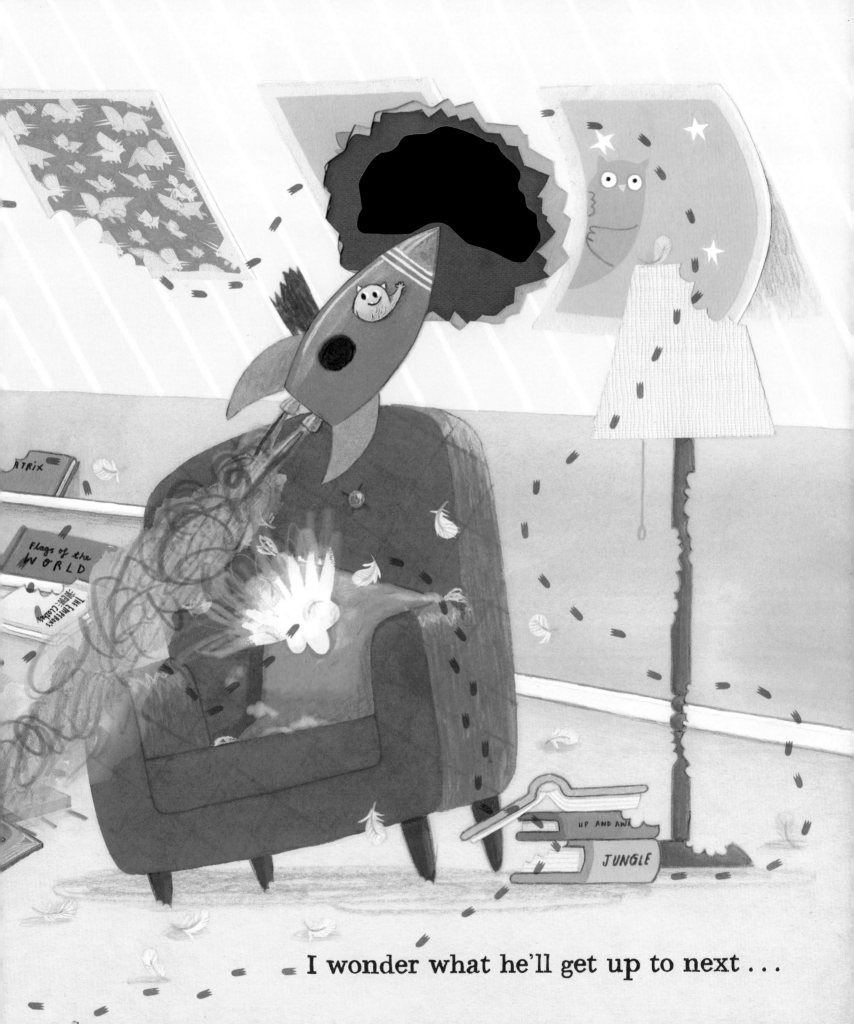

I wonder what he'll get up to next . . .